THE GHOST OF DR. MOLD

text by Roberto Pavanello
translated by Marco Zeni

STONE ARCH BOOKS
a capstone imprint

First published in the United States in 2013
by Stone Arch Books
A Capstone Imprint
1710 Roe Crest Drive
North Mankato, Minnesota 56003
www.capstonepub.com

Text by Roberto Pavanello
Original cover and illustrations by Blasco Pisapia and Pamela Brughera
Graphic Project by Laura Zuccotti and Gioia Giunchi

Original Title: IL FANTASMA DEL DOTTOR MUFFA

Translation by: Marco Zeni

www.batpat.it

LIbrary of Congress Cataloging-in-Publication Data is available on the Library of Congress website.

Library Binding: 978-1-4342-3834-4
e-baook PDF: 978-1-4342-4628-8

Summary: Echo and the Bat Pack solve an ancient mystery. But they aren't the only ones on the case — there's a ghost there as well!

Designer: Emily Harris
Production Specialist: Michelle Biedscheid

Printed in the United States of America in North Mankato, Minnesota.
042012 006682CGF12

TABLE OF CONTENTS

Hello there!

I'm your friend Echo, here to tell you about one of the Bat Pack's adventures!

Do you know what I do for a living? I'm a writer, and scary stories are my specialty. Creepy stories about witches, ghosts, and graveyards. But I'll tell you a secret — I am a real scaredy-bat!

First of all, let me introduce you to the Bat Pack. These are my friends. . . .

Becca

Age: 10

Loves all animals (especially bats!)

Excellent at bandaging broken wings

Michael

Age: 12

Smart, thoughtful, and good at solving problems

Doesn't take no for an answer

Tyler

Age: 11

Computer genius

Funny and adventurous, but scared of his own shadow

Dear fans of scary stories,

Have you ever had those terrible red pimples that make you look like a toad with measles? I'll bet you have. They're pretty common. But what about a case of blue pimples? I bet you've never had those!

Well, that's exactly what happened to Becca. And to a certain baron's daughter a few centuries before. Those blue pimples are the reason I had to learn to use a cell phone, take nighttime tours in haunted castles, and meet a very absent-minded (and very dead!) doctor.

On the upside, those blue pimples gave me the chance to see my old teacher again. I know that bats don't usually go to school, but my

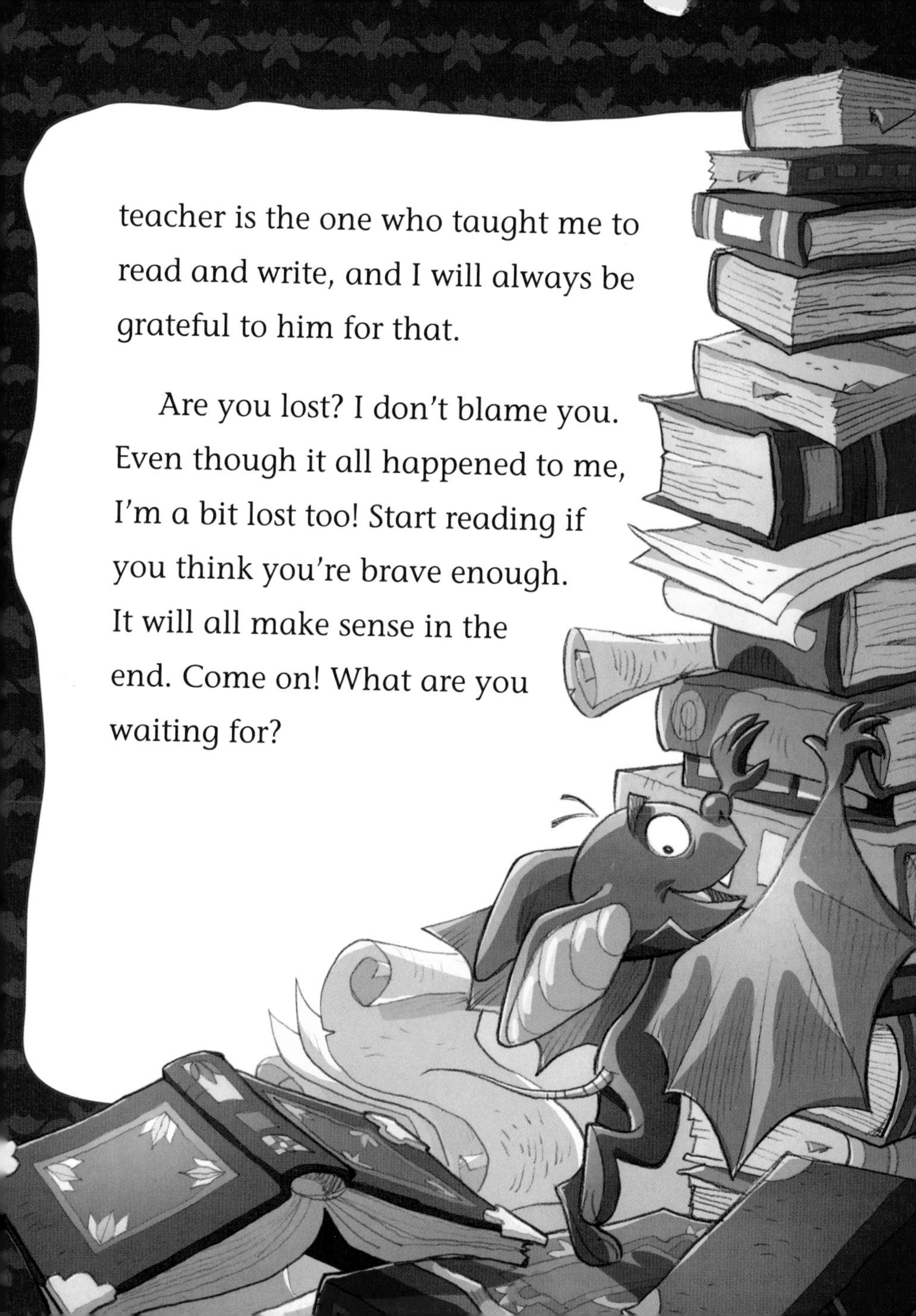

teacher is the one who taught me to read and write, and I will always be grateful to him for that.

Are you lost? I don't blame you. Even though it all happened to me, I'm a bit lost too! Start reading if you think you're brave enough. It will all make sense in the end. Come on! What are you waiting for?

Chapter 1

A Clumsy Mailman

It was a lazy, gray Sunday morning in Fogville when our latest adventure began. I had just come in from one of my night flights and gone up to the attic to crawl into bed. Bats sleep during the day, you know. Even living with humans couldn't change that fact!

The rest of the Silver family was still sound asleep too. Everyone except for Becca, that is. She had been up since 7 a.m. I swear, that girl never sleeps! She had already exercised, taken a shower, eaten breakfast, and had even found the time to flip through the *Fogville Echo*. What an overachiever!

Becca was still sitting in the kitchen reading the newspaper when something outside suddenly caught her attention. There was a pigeon falling from the sky! The poor bird was frantically flapping his wings, trying to slow down. But it was no use. He crashed straight into the front door of the Silvers' house.

If I'd been there, I could have told you that pigeon made a typical beginner's mistake. The braking maneuver is one of the first things I learned from my cousin Limp Wing! He's an accomplished member of the Aerobatic Display Team, you know!

Becca immediately rushed outside to check on the poor bird.

The pigeon stood up awkwardly and glanced around, looking confused. Not that I blame him. That collision must have rattled his brain!

"Hey! Are you okay, little guy?" Becca asked worriedly.

The little animal jolted in fear. He immediately lost his balance again and tumbled backward. He sat there looking stunned.

Leaning down, Becca gently picked the pigeon up and cradled him in her arms. That girl has never met an animal she didn't love — lucky for me!

As she held him, Becca noticed a tiny roll of paper tied to the bird's leg. He was a carrier pigeon! But who had sent him?

"What do you have here?" Becca asked. She reached down and untied the roll of paper from the bird's leg.

Scrawled across the front of the piece of paper were the words, "To Echo."

"Echo?" Becca said in surprise. "Our Echo? Who would be sending him mail?"

Suddenly the bird leaped out of Becca's hands. Before she could even react, he hopped around like a crazed kangaroo and took a few steps, getting a running start. Then he took flight, swerving through the sky.

Becca stood outside watching until the bird was just a tiny dark spot on the horizon.

I, of course, didn't see any of this. I was still sound asleep, hanging upside down from a ceiling beam in the attic like a responsible bat. But Becca made sure I heard every detail.

I was abruptly awakened when she came charging up the stairs to the attic. She stormed into my room yelling, "MAIL FOR ECHO! MAIL FOR ECHO!" at the top of her lungs.

I was so startled that I almost fell off my perch! I really hate being woken up like that, especially when I'm in the middle of fluttering around the dream world, but the moment I heard those words, I opened my eyes wide. There was only one person in the whole wide world who would be sending me mail, and I hadn't heard from him in years.

Chapter 2

Tear-Soaked Tissues

My eyes were still too tired from my abrupt wake-up call to focus on the words, so I asked Becca to read the message for me. It said:

Dear Echo,

If you are reading this, it means that my old carrier pigeon Gideon managed to get to you, and for that I am grateful. I am badly in need of your help. For the past month, strange things have been happening in my library. At night, someone has been rummaging through my books and scattering them throughout the hallways! Whoever it is has been making a terrible mess!

Last night, however, things got much worse. An entire room in the library was turned inside out! Now the famous 18th-century essay "The Science of Hydraulics" by Fritz Mineralwasser is missing! I don't know what to do!

The library director was furious when I told him what had happened. He told me that I am too old for this job and threatened to fire me if I don't find the missing book.

That's why I thought of you. You've always been so good at solving mysteries. After all, you're a mystery writer! If we work together, maybe we can uncover the identity of this criminal and bring him to justice. My job depends on it!

Please fly over here as soon as you can. Without your help, I fear it might be too late for me!

Your teacher,

Arthur

By the time Becca was finished reading the letter, I was crying like a baby.

"Echo, what's the matter?" Becca asked, looking concerned. "Who is this Arthur guy?"

But it was no use. I was sobbing so loudly that I couldn't even talk. But my crying did manage to wake up Tyler and Michael. Both boys came running upstairs to the attic.

"What's going on?" Michael asked, putting on his glasses.

Tyler, who still looked half asleep, was less concerned. "Jeez, Echo! I was sleeping, you know!" he complained. "Do you think you could you keep it down a little?"

"Tyler, be nice!" Becca snapped, glaring at her brother. "Can't you see how upset Echo is?"

Becca turned back to me and held out a tissue. "Calm down, Echo," she said. "What's the problem?"

I took a tissue from Becca's hands and blew my nose loudly. "Do you remember how I told you that I used to live in the attic of an old

library?" I asked. "I used to secretly listen to the librarian when he read stories to the children. We eventually became friends. He's the one who taught me how to read and write."

"And the letter is from the librarian?" Michael guessed.

"Yes! And now he's in trouble!" I said. "I have to fly over there immediately! He needs my help right away!"

"Take it easy, Echo," Michael said. "Maybe we can help you. Where exactly does this guy Arthur live?"

"He lives in Castlerock," I replied. "It's not too far away."

"Castlerock?" Becca repeated. "The same Castlerock that's also known as Ghost Castle?"

"That's the one," I replied.

"We've been up for less than ten minutes and you're already talking ghosts?" Tyler interrupted. "This has to be a new record."

"It's just a legend, Tyler," Michael said. "Relax. There's nothing to be afraid of."

Tyler ignored him. "Echo, do you think you

can wait thirty minutes before you head off in search of trouble?" he asked.

"I guess," I said. "But why?"

"I have to charge your Bat-Phone," Tyler said with a grin.

Chapter 3

The Bat-Phone

What is a Bat-Phone, you ask? It's a bat-sized cell phone, of course! It was Tyler's latest invention, made just for yours truly.

"With this, we can keep in touch even if we're miles apart," Tyler explained, holding up a tiny phone. "What do you think?"

"I think you must be out of your mind!" I told him. "How on earth do you expect me to use that?"

Tyler ignored my protests and showed me how to work the phone. A few minutes later, I became the first bat in history to ever send a text message.

I was thrilled! After all, my little sister Marshmallow must have told me a hundred times, "Keep up with new technology or you'll become ancient mythology!"

"Give us a call as soon as you get there," Becca told me.

"We'll try to come meet you as soon as possible," Michael promised.

With that, I hugged my friends one by one and took off for Castlerock.

* * *

The sun had just set when I finally arrived at

Castlerock. I had been flying for so long that my wings felt like stone.

Castlerock was perched at the very top of a steep hill, overlooking the town below. As I flew overhead, I noticed that the houses surrounding the castle looked like a brood of chicks crouched under their mother hen. How's that for a simile? Am I a great writer or what?

As I flew closer, I recognized the library building. My old home! I flew to the only lit window. Inside, I could see my old friend Arthur standing in front of a messy bookshelf, picking up books from the floor and shaking his head. Gideon, the old carrier pigeon that had delivered Arthur's letter, was sleeping on his shoulder.

I tapped softly on the glass pane. When Arthur saw me, he flung open the window and gave me a crushing hug. By the time he let go of me, he was close to tears.

"Echo! It's so good to see you after all these years!" he exclaimed. He held me out in front of him. "Let me take a look at you! My, how you've grown! You're certainly wearing some fashionable clothes these days!"

"Oh, I have my friend Becca to thank for that," I said. "You remember her. I wrote about the Silver family in my letters."

"Of course," Arthur replied, nodding. "She's one of the three children you live with. Thank you so much for coming, Echo. I can't tell you how much I appreciate it."

"I could never abandon you when you needed me," I said. "Not after all you've done for me! We'll catch this scoundrel. You have my word!"

"Just look at this mess!" Arthur said, gesturing to the books scattered across the floor.

He shook his head sadly. "And it's been getting worse every night! I don't know what to do. I'm at my wit's end!"

Arthur took a deep breath to calm himself. "Anyway, you must be exhausted. Would you like something to eat?"

"Do you still have those yummy blueberry scones?" I asked.

"Of course!" Arthur replied. "They were always your favorite." He pulled out the same old tin I remembered and set it out for me.

I bit into the scone and was immediately hit by a flood of memories. I had spent hours on end in that same room, listening to Arthur read. There was only one thing missing.

The words came out of my mouth so naturally that I almost didn't realize I'd said them. "Arthur, would you tell me a story?"

Chapter 4

Once Upon a Time

"Do you remember the story of Dr. Mold?" Arthur asked.

I nodded. "It used to be one of my favorites when I was younger!" I replied.

"Well, Dr. Mold's real name was actually Dr. Allen Bick," Arthur continued. "He was a terribly absent-minded man, but he was also famous for being an incredible healer. As soon as Baron MacTherry, the owner of Castlerock, heard of Dr. Bick's talents, he made him his personal physician. Dr. Bick also had an assistant named Rodrigo. Rodrigo was always plotting behind Dr. Bick's back. You see, he wanted the position of personal physician for himself."

I nodded, completely spellbound by Arthur's story.

"Suddenly, Greta, the Baron's beautiful daughter, caught a terrible skin disease called blueberry scrofula," Arthur said. "Her face was covered with blue spots! Her mother took her to several doctors, but no one could find a cure. They tried the weirdest remedies: hot snakeskin compresses, mustard hair ointments, even ice-cold baths in blueberry shakes! But Greta's pimples remained blue."

"Then," Arthur told me, "the baron sent for Dr. Bick. He promised to pay him in gold if he could cure Greta."

"Did he agree to see her?" I asked.

Arthur nodded. "Dr. Bick visited Greta and then he and Rodrigo locked themselves in his laboratory to find a cure. He worked all night.

But his attempt at curing Greta was a disaster. First, she turned green, then brown, and finally *completely* blue! The baron was furious. He had the doctor locked up in the tower prison and ordered that his daughter's face be covered with a dark shawl."

"That's terrible!" I exclaimed.

"Several days later, Rodrigo went to see the baron again," Arthur continued. "He claimed he'd done new research and found the right cure for Greta. At first, the baron didn't believe Rodrigo. But Rodrigo was insistent. He even agreed that the baron could lock him up in the tower with Dr. Mold if his cure didn't work. But there was another side to the deal. If the potion did work, Rodrigo wanted to be the baron's new family physician. The baron thought about it and accepted the offer. And he was right to do so, because the cure was a success.

Greta recovered completely, and Rodrigo took Dr. Mold's place, just as they'd agreed. Poor Dr. Mold was left to rot in the tower cell until the end of his days. His restless ghost has been haunting the castle since then."

When he finished his story, Arthur glanced over at me. But the long flight had been too much for me. I was sound asleep.

Arthur sighed and gently covered me up with his jacket. Then he stood up and got to work putting the old books back in their places.

Chapter 5

A Happy Family Trip

In the middle of the night, loud noises woke me up. I could hear stomping, thumping noises, and Arthur's voice shouting, "Stop! Show your face, you coward! I said stop!"

I rushed over in the blink of an eye and found him standing in front of an old cabinet with glass doors. The glass doors had been opened and the cabinet was empty. The mysterious night visitor had struck again!

That night, I sent Tyler the first animal text in history using my Bat-Phone. It read, "GET HERE AS SOON AS POSSIBLE. I NEED HELP!"

* * *

That afternoon, I helped Arthur put the books back in their places and made sure that he got some rest. I kept watch all night and used the opportunity to take a look around my old home. There were so many memories!

The next morning, my Bat-Phone chimed, announcing the arrival of a text. It was from Michael.

"WE ARE STANDING IN FRONT OF THE CASTLE. FLY OVER HERE. GUIDED TOUR STARTS IN 10 MINUTES."

I had underestimated my friends' powers of persuasion. They'd started trying to convince poor Mr. Silver (who had already been dreaming of a quiet couch-potato weekend) as soon as I texted them the night before.

"Hey, Dad," Becca had said. "Did you know you've never taken us to see Castlerock? What do you think about going there tomorrow?"

"I've been waiting to see it for years!" Michael had added. "The castle was the setting

for Edgar Allan Poultry's novel *Blueberry Face*. It's one of my favorite stories!"

Even Mrs. Silver had chimed in. "It sounds like a good idea, George. Besides, I just saw an ad the other day that children 12 years old and younger stay for free. It'll be fun!"

Poor Mr. Silver was outnumbered. But the moment he saw me gliding toward them the next day, he knew something was up.

"Echo?" he said. "What are you doing here? What is this all really about?"

"It's all my fault, Mr. Silver," I tried to explain. "I asked your children to come here."

"Why?" Mr. Silver demanded.

I had to think quickly. After all, I couldn't exactly say that I had called them there to help me catch a thief!

"Because . . . because I wanted you to see where I used to live," I answered. I smiled as sincerely as I could.

Mr. Silver started mumbling something, but fortunately, the young man who was going to be our guide arrived, and the castle tour began.

Chapter 6

Sneeze Fountain

When the tour began, I hid inside Becca's backpack as usual to avoid scaring the rest of the tourists. (I have to hide there most of the time when we go out in public. I'll never understand why bats are so scary to you humans!) I listened carefully to our tour guide as he explained Castlerock's history.

"Castlerock dates back to the 14th century," the guide told us. "The castle has stayed mostly the same since it was built, but it underwent dramatic changes between 1733 and 1735, after Baron MacTherry bought it."

As our guide spoke, we crossed a huge garden filled with fountains and waterfalls. I peeked out of Becca's backpack as the group came to a stop in front of an enormous pink marble shell that sprayed water into a larger pool. It was magnificent!

"The elegant fountains that you see were one of Baron MacTherry's passions," our guide explained. "This one was called 'The Fountain of Eternal Youth.'"

"Does it work?" Tyler asked, leaning into the fountain.

"I have no idea," the guide said, smiling. "But what I do know is that Dr. Mold himself, the baron's unlucky personal physician, designed this fountain, as well as the others you'll see around the cas —"

Before the guide could finish his sentence, Tyler fell into the pool, splashing water on most of the other visitors.

"I'm sorry . . . *ptooey,*" Tyler mumbled, spitting water out of his mouth and struggling to climb out of the fountain. "I just wanted . . . *ptooey* . . .

to take a sip . . . you know to stay young . . . aaa . . . tchoo!"

Mr. Silver leaned over and helped pull Tyler out of the water, while Mrs. Silver tried to find something to help him dry off. Michael, Becca, and I could barely control our laughter.

Once Tyler was somewhat dry, we climbed the spiral staircase that led to the infamous

cell on the tower's top floor. Our tour guide told us Dr. Mold's sad story, and then stopped in front of an old door with a peephole. The door was securely blocked by thick iron bar.

"The room that you'll see behind this door used to be Dr. Mold's laboratory," our guide explained. "After the disaster with his daughter, Greta, the baron had it turned into a prison cell. The doctor was kept prisoner here until the day he died. Rumor has it that humidity in the room was so high that mold eventually covered the poor doctor from head to toe. That's how he got his nickname. According to the legend, Dr. Mold's ghost appears every night and wanders around the castle, wailing."

When no one was looking, I managed to pop my head out of Becca's backpack and sneak a peek into the small room. Inside there was a bed, several shelves full of books, and a table covered with dusty vials. All the vials were wrapped in a tangle of cobwebs and filled with moldy liquids. Yuck!

"There's no need to be scared," our guide reassured us. "It goes without saying that this is only a legend. I'm sure those of you planning to spend the night here will have a restful night's sleep."

Despite the guide's reassurances, something

told me that I wouldn't be sleeping at all that night.

"Does anyone have any questions?" the guide asked.

I had plenty of questions, but I figured our guide would have a hard time answering a talking bat hidden in a little girl's backpack.

And besides, it was time for the Silver kids to meet Arthur.

Chapter 7

Chicken Hunting

We managed to break away from Mr. and Mrs. Silver by telling them that we needed to go back to the hotel to get changed before dinner. We promised to meet them in the dining room to eat later that night.

Tyler was more than happy with the idea. He couldn't wait to get rid of his wet clothes. Needless to say, he was not happy when I directed them toward the library instead.

"Hey, where are we going? I thought we were going back to the hotel to change!" he complained.

"Not now, Tyler," Becca said. "We have to meet with Arthur at the library and make it back to the hotel before Mom and Dad do. Now hurry up!"

"But I have water in my underwear!" Tyler whined.

"Well, you should have thought about that before you went swimming in the fountain," Becca told him.

When we arrived at the library, Arthur was already standing by the door, waiting for us. Old Gideon was asleep on his shoulder as usual.

"Come in, come in!" Arthur said. "It's so nice to finally meet all of you. Any friends of Echo's are friends of mine!"

Arthur offered us tea and blueberry biscuits. Then we all sat down while he filled the Silver kids in on what had been happening around Castlerock.

"That's aaa . . . chooooooo!" Tyler sneezed.

"There's only one thing to do," Michael said. "We'll have to catch the thief in the act."

"You think I haven't already tried that?"

Arthur replied. "Running after a thief at my age isn't exactly easy!"

"There are four of us now," Michael said. "And one of us can fly. We'll catch that thief, no problem!"

As he spoke, Michael's glasses started to fog up. He took them off to clean them.

I was glad Michael was so confident, but I was still a little worried. I knew all too well that when Michael's glasses fogged up like that, trouble was on its way for the Bat Pack!

"But what if the thief does to us what he did to the books?" Tyler asked. "Haven't we had enough bad luck? I've already caught a col . . . achoo!"

Michael ignored his brother's complaints. "Let's plan to meet in front of the library tonight at midnight," he said. "Arthur, can you let us in? Then we can lock the door behind us. All the other exits will be locked too."

"Do you really think that's necessary?" Tyler whimpered, looking extremely nervous. "That means we'll be trapped!"

"Yes, but so will the thief!" Michael replied, grinning triumphantly.

* * *

We made it back to the hotel with only moments to spare. As we hurried in the front door and up to our rooms, we saw Mr. and Mrs. Silver walking in behind us.

Everyone quickly changed for dinner. Tyler was especially grateful to finally get out of his wet clothes! Then we hurried down to the dining room to meet Mr. and Mrs. Silver.

Michael, Tyler, and Becca were starving after our exciting day and practically devoured their food. I stayed hidden inside Rebecca's backpack and ate what she passed me.

After dinner, we excused ourselves. "It's been such a long day," Becca told her parents, pretending to yawn. "I think we're just going to go to bed early."

"Good idea," Michael agreed. "I'm exhausted!"

We hurried back up to our room and waited until it was time to leave. At 11:45 p.m., the Silver kids and I snuck out of the hotel and headed back to Castlerock to meet Arthur.

When we arrived at 11:55 p.m., Arthur was waiting out front to let us into the library.

And at midnight sharp, our hunt for the book thief began!

Chapter 8

Get the Green Ghost!

We decided that we'd better keep the lights off so we didn't give away our location, but after Tyler tripped and fell for the third time in a row, we had to change our plans. I flipped open my Bat-Phone and silently took the lead, guiding the rest of the group using the bluish glow of the display.

"Once again, my inventions save the . . . achoo!" Tyler said.

"Stop sneezing, Tyler," Becca complained. "You're going to lead the thief right to us if you keep making so much noise!"

"Both of you, shush!" Michael said. "I think there's someone over there. Look!"

At the end of the hallway, we could just make out a faint glow coming from the library.

"What . . . what is that?" Tyler stammered nervously.

"I can't tell from here," Michael replied. "Someone should go check it out." At his words, all three of the Silver kids turned to look at me expectantly.

I knew what was coming. "You were going to ask me, weren't you?" I said. "Just because I'm small and can fly and blah-blah-blah." I sighed. "All right, fine, I'll go!"

I wasn't exactly thrilled at the thought of finding myself face to face with a criminal, especially when I was flying solo, so I kept very close to the ceiling as I crept closer to the library.

My little heart was beating like crazy as I flew silently inside. There was someone standing in front of the bookcase!

I almost had a heart attack when I realized that the glowing green guy in front of me was floating rather than standing! He was wearing an old-fashioned coat, a pair of tattered-looking buckle shoes, and a worn-out hat. A pair of glasses hung from a lock of green hair — green just like the layer of mold that covered him from head to toe.

That must be the ghost of Dr. Mold! I thought, shuddering.

The ghost pulled book after book off the shelf,

carefully flipping through each one. He seemed to be looking for something. But whatever it was, he couldn't seem to find it. He kept repeating, "Where did I put it? Oh, where did I put it!" before hurling each book to the floor.

My Bat-Phone suddenly chimed loudly in the silence. It was a text from Tyler asking where I was!

The ghost started in surprise. Looking over his shoulder, he saw me and said, "Rodrigo? Is that you?"

I didn't even have time to reply before the ghost threw a book at me and flew away. I immediately rushed after him.

The Silver kids saw me and joined the race. But that guy was faster than a speeding bullet! I could hear Michael yelling, "Stop running! There's no way out of here!"

"We won't hurt you!" Becca yelled.

"Please stop running! I'm tired!" yelled Tyler.

I flew after them. It was obvious that my friends didn't know what they were dealing with.

Becca suddenly found herself standing in front of the ghost. She tried to stop him, but being a ghost (how could they not see that!?), he passed right through her. As he did, he shouted, "May you come down with scarlet fever, whooping cough, blueberry scrofula!"

The ghost flew toward the upper floor. Michael and I were hot on his heels. When he realized that he'd reached a dead end, the ghost turned around and faced us. "What do you want from me?" he yelled.

"We just want to help you," Michael said calmly. Judging from the look on his face, I

could tell he was starting to realize that we were not dealing with an ordinary thief.

"No one can help me!" the ghost moaned. "No one!"

With that, the ghost flew straight through the

wall and disappeared. Michael stared at me in shock. "That was a . . . a . . ." he stuttered.

"A ghost!" I finished for him. At that point, I just couldn't keep it a secret anymore.

There was nothing else we could do. Michael and I walked back and found Tyler at the bottom of the stairs. He was holding on to Becca, who was pale and shaking like a leaf. Even worse, weird pimples were popping up all over her face.

Chapter 9

A Great Disease!

The next morning, Becca's face was still covered with blue pimples. It goes without saying that we hadn't told Mr. and Mrs. Silver what had happened, so they assumed Becca's pimples were some unusual form of the measles. They insisted on taking her to the emergency room. Unfortunately, even the doctor was stumped.

"I've never seen anything like this," the

frustrated doctor said. "I think I should let my colleague take a look at your daughter. I'll go get him."

A few minutes later, a short, smiling man entered the room. "I'm Dr. Black," he introduced himself. "Dr. Neil Black the third."

The moment I saw the doctor's face, I wanted to jump out of the hood of Tyler's sweater. He could have been the ghost's twin! And that name . . . Neil Black. It sounded familiar somehow.

As soon as he saw Becca's face, the doctor's mouth dropped open.

"Your pimples are . . . are . . . blue!" he stammered. "That's great!"

"What's so great about them?" Becca snapped at him.

"Oh, I'm sorry, dear," the doctor replied, chuckling. "It's just that this is the very first case I've seen, and I'm a little excited!"

"First case of what?" an alarmed Mrs. Silver asked.

"Of blue disease, of course!" Dr. Black replied. "It's one of the oldest and most unusual contagious diseases. It used to be called blueberry scrofula."

By my grandpa's sonar! That was the same disease that Arthur had mentioned in his story! At that point, I had no more doubts. I waited until Becca and her parents had left the room, and then I told Tyler and Michael my suspicions.

"Dr. Black is a distant relative of Dr. Mold," I said. "I'm sure of it!"

"How can you be so sure?" Tyler asked, looking confused.

"Are you telling me you didn't notice the resemblance between him and the ghost we saw yesterday? Besides, Arthur told me that Dr. Mold's real name was Allen Bick," I said. "Take a look at this."

I grabbed a piece of paper and wrote down both names for them. Sometimes being able to write comes in really handy! I held it out to Michael and Tyler to show them what I'd realized — both names were made up of the exact same letters!

"Of course! You're a genius, Echo!" Michael exclaimed.

"And you heard the doctor. Becca caught the same disease the girl in the legend did," I said.

"Oh, yeah," Tyler said sternly. "The 'Mulberry Brofula'!"

"There's only one thing to do," Michael said. "We have to talk with the person directly involved."

We set off to find Dr. Black. We must have looked all over the hospital for him! Finally we spotted the doctor just as he was about to step into an elevator.

"Hello, boys. Are you looking for the exit?" Dr. Black asked, smiling.

"Not exactly. . . ." Tyler muttered.

"What can I help you with?" Dr. Black asked.

"We're looking for a relative of Dr. Allen Bick," Michael said. "Do you by any chance know him?"

The doctor stared at us, flabbergasted. Then he smiled again and said, "We'd better talk about this someplace quiet. Let's go to my office."

Chapter 10

Mulberry Brofula

Once we were in his office, Dr. Black asked us to take a seat. Then he spoke as bluntly as Michael had.

"It's true," he admitted. "I am a descendant of Dr. Allen Bick. I came here a few months ago and changed my last name to keep it a secret. I'm investigating the real story behind what happened to my great-uncle."

I knew I had to tell the doctor what I'd seen

the night before, so I wiggled out of the hood of Tyler's sweatshirt.

"Oh, my!" the doctor gasped. "That's a bat!"

"A *bat sapiens* if you don't mind!" I snapped back, offended.

"And it can talk!" Dr. Black exclaimed.

"Quite well, thank you," I replied. "It shouldn't come as that big of a surprise. After all, you have a relative who's a ghost! You must be used to strange things."

I told the doctor about Arthur, about the thief that had been ransacking the library, and about the story Arthur had told me the night before. The doctor nodded at every sentence.

When I got to the part about the blueberry scrofula, Dr. Black suddenly leaped out of his chair.

"So my information was right!" he exclaimed. "And that's the same disease your sister has. How is that possible?"

"We had a face-to-face encounter with your great-uncle last night," Michael told him. "And when Becca was trying to stop him, he called her all kinds of names."

"I remember that!" Tyler interrupted. "He yelled, 'May you come down with starlet fever, hopping cough, mulberry brofula!' Or something like that, I think."

"I see," the doctor replied slowly. "I think I know how to cure your sister, but I might need your help."

"What do you mean?" Michael asked.

"I think my great-uncle was unfairly imprisoned," Dr. Black told us. "I've done quite a bit of research, and from what I can tell, he actually did find a cure for the baron's daughter. However, since he was a bit of a scatterbrain, there's a good chance he may have lost the formula or hidden it somewhere. I want to find it! That will help me prove his innocence. That's where you and your friend Arthur come in."

Suddenly, something crashed into the windowpane. We all turned to see what it

was. Gideon was lying half unconscious on the windowsill. He had another message from Arthur tied to his leg. This time, the message read:

Come to the library immediately! You won't believe what I've found!

Chapter 11

Even Walls Crumble

Arthur was waiting impatiently when we arrived at the library. He barely gave us time to take a breath before ushering us toward one of the library's old wooden bookcases.

There were books scattered all over the floor as usual, but this time Arthur didn't look concerned. Quite the opposite, in fact. He just kept smiling and repeating, "I knew it! I knew it!"

Turning on his flashlight, he showed us what had him so excited. At the back of the bookcase, he had unearthed a small door that had been hidden behind the books. It was just big enough for a person to crawl through.

"Follow me," Arthur said.

We crawled through the tight opening and discovered a narrow set of stairs. None of us had any idea where the stairs led. None of us except

Arthur, who kept mumbling, "I knew that there had to be a passage."

We reached the top of the stairs and found a trapdoor blocking our way.

"Great. Now where do we go?" Tyler muttered. "I don't want to be stuck back here!"

"Do you know what's behind that door?" Michael asked, sounding curious.

"I have a pretty good idea," Arthur answered.

Tyler cut him short. "Can we save this guessing for later? It's pretty tight in here."

Arthur opened the trapdoor, and we found ourselves standing in front of an old brick wall.

"That's impossible!" Arthur gasped. "What are we going to do now?"

"We'll knock it down!" I immediately replied.

"That's a great idea!" Tyler replied sarcastically. "Let me see if I have my pickax with me."

"We won't need that," I said, pressing my ear against the wall and tapping it with my fingers. "We just need to find the wall's weak spot. And then . . . there! I found it!"

I spun myself around, threw a solid kick, and the wall crumbled.

"Where did you learn to do that?" Tyler asked, his eyes wide with disbelief.

"It's an old trick I learned from my cousin Limp Wing," I explained.

When the dust had settled, we saw what had been hidden behind the brick wall — a tiny door that had been closed for centuries. Can you guess where it led?

Into Dr. Mold's laboratory, of course! We had discovered a secret passageway into his tower cell.

"How is it possible that no one has discovered this passage before?" Michael asked.

"Ancient documents say that there were passages connecting the library to some of the other rooms in the castle," Arthur replied. "Obviously, one of them connected the library to the doctor's laboratory. Before it became his prison, that is."

"That's right!" Michael exclaimed. "I forgot, our tour guide told us that Dr. Mold was locked up in his lab. They must have walled up the old library passage to prevent him from running away."

"Then he must have hidden this here," Tyler added, pulling a small leather-bound notebook

from a crack in the wall. He carefully held it out and blew the dust off of it.

We all read the words that were clearly written on its cover. "DIARY OF A PRISONER."

Chapter 12

Betrayal! Betrayal!

You should have seen Arthur's face when he realized what we'd found! He almost started crying tears of joy.

"This is Dr. Mold's journal!" he exclaimed. "What an amazing discovery!" He started flipping through the pages very carefully. Then he began to read aloud from the journal. The magic of his voice seemed to take us back in time to when the words had been written.

"Whoever finds this journal, may he know that I concealed it so that it would not fall into the hands of evil Baron MacTherry, the wicked man who had me locked up in this humid prison," Arthur read aloud. "The baron refused to believe me when I tried to tell him the truth. He sentenced me before even hearing me out. But you, who now read my words, please hear my story before you judge me."

"I have goose bumps!" Tyler exclaimed. "This is like a scary movie! Does anyone have any popcorn?"

"Knock it off, Tyler!" Michael said. "Keep reading, Arthur."

"Let it be known that I wasn't the one responsible for poisoning the baron's daughter,"

Arthur read. "It was another man, one who schemed against me behind my back. A man I trusted, who betrayed me out of sheer ambition, even though I loved him like a son and taught him everything I knew. It was Rodrigo Mendez de la Rodilla, my personal assistant."

"I knew it!" I exclaimed. "I knew Dr. Mold wasn't responsible!" I leaned over Arthur's shoulder to get a better look at Dr. Mold's journal. This is what he had written:

When I examined the baron's daughter, Greta, I immediately diagnosed her with a rare form of blue disease. I spent a sleepless night working in my laboratory with Rodrigo. He came up with several useful suggestions about how to write the formula for the medication. We worked and worked until we found the right combination. I was certain that I had found the cure.

I was getting ready to return to Greta's room to

give her the cure I'd created when Rodrigo stopped me. He suggested that I write down the formula for the medication first. That way I could be sure nothing would be forgotten. He offered to take the medication to Greta himself.

Totally unaware of his plot, I handed him the cure I'd created and told him to give Greta half of the available dosage. Then I returned to my laboratory.

I was so tired that I decided to rest my eyes for a moment. But I must have fallen asleep as soon as I laid my head on the table. Thirty minutes later, I was woken by desperate screaming coming from Greta's room.

I immediately ran downstairs and discovered a disaster. Her face had turned completely blue! I glanced at Rodrigo, who acted shocked. I grabbed the vial that still held half the medication and hurried back to my laboratory.

When I tested the remaining liquid, I realized that someone had changed the ingredients. I immediately suspected my young assistant. I was about to go demand an explanation when the baron's guards suddenly burst into my laboratory and arrested me.

I protested that I was innocent, but my accusations against Rodrigo were in vain. No one believed me. A few days later, Rodrigo went to the

baron and asked for permission to try to cure Greta on his own. He used the formula I'd written down. When it worked, he became the baron's personal physician and Greta's husband at the same time. I was done for. However, I managed to do one final thing before the baron ordered the passage to the library be closed. I copied the original formula for the medicine and hid it in one of those old books.

Find it for me, you who are reading these words, and redeem my name. No other hope comforts me.

Dr. Allen Bick

"That's it!" Michael exclaimed. "That must be what the ghost has been looking for in the library. He hid the formula in one of those books!"

Chapter 13

A Nice Blue Face

"Where on earth have you been?" Mr. Silver demanded when we arrived at the hotel. "And why are you all covered in dust?"

"We were so worried!" Mrs. Silver added.

"Well, um . . . Echo was showing us the old attic where he used to live!" Tyler lied.

"How is Becca feeling?" Michael asked, clearly trying to change the subject. "Does she look any better?"

“Her condition is stable, but the doctors have no idea how to help her,” Mrs. Silver replied, shaking her head.

We ate lunch in silence and then hurried back to our room. There were so many questions bouncing around in our heads. Why couldn’t the ghost find the formula he had hidden? Would we have better luck? Would it even work against the blue disease Becca had contracted?

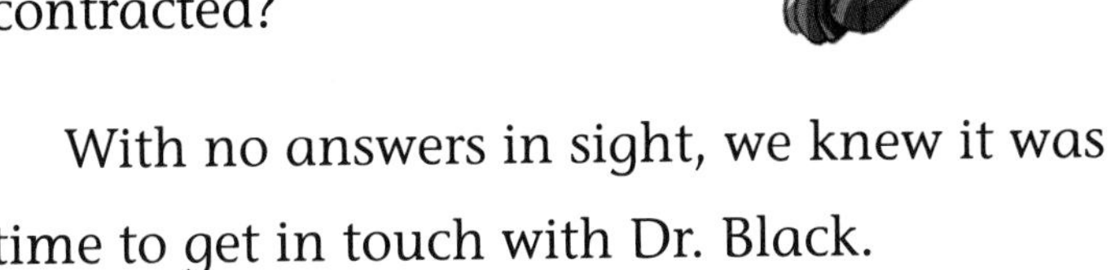

With no answers in sight, we knew it was time to get in touch with Dr. Black.

Just then, my Bat-Phone buzzed with a text message from Becca. It read:

"DID YOU FORGET ABOUT ME? GET OVER HERE RIGHT AWAY. I WANT TO KNOW WHAT'S GOING ON!"

"It's about time you showed up!" Becca said when we walked into her hospital room. Her face was still covered with blue dots.

"Looking good, Becca," Tyler said. "Blue pimples are really your look."

Becca was about to throw a pillow at her brother when Dr. Black walked in.

"Excellent! I was looking for you three!" the doctor said when he saw us. "Do you have any news?"

"Great news," Michael answered. "We might have found the cure for the blue disease, and it's all thanks to your great-uncle!"

"Would someone please tell me what's going on?" Becca protested. "In case you've forgotten, I'm the one who looks like a Dalmatian!"

We told Becca and Dr. Black about the secret passageway we'd discovered in the library, as well as Dr. Mold's journal.

"I knew that something wasn't right!" Dr. Black exclaimed. "All we have to do now is to find the formula!"

"That's not exactly going to be easy," Michael said. "The library has more than thirty thousand books! It's like looking for a needle in a haystack!"

"And not even your great-uncle has been able to find it so far!" Becca added.

"Well, if he's anything like me, I can't blame him," Tyler interrupted. "The other day I was looking for one of my sneakers, and do you know where I found it? In the freezer!"

"Arthur did tell me that Dr. Mold was a bit absentminded," I said. "For all we know, the formula could be in one of those fountains in the garden instead of in one of the books!"

Michael stared at me wide-eyed. “Of course! The fountains!” he said. “Echo, you’re a genius! Come on! There’s no time to waste!”

“Hey! I want to come with you! No fair!” Becca said as everyone, including Dr. Black, rushed out of the room.

I really wanted to keep her company, but I didn’t have a choice. I knew they would need me to solve that mystery.

Chapter 14

Hey, Echo...

"Do you really think that my great-uncle hid the formula in one of the fountains?" Dr. Black asked, running after Michael.

"Of course not," Michael said. "That would be ridiculous. But I just remembered something our tour guide said about the fountains your great-uncle designed."

"And?" Dr. Black asked. "What does that have to do with anything?"

"You'll see," Michael said. "I think this could help us solve our mystery. But I need to ask Arthur a question. Let's get back to the library."

Arthur was waiting for us with a worried look on his face when we arrived.

Michael immediately started asking questions. "Arthur, does the library have a section on hydraulics?" he asked.

"Of course it does," Arthur said. "In fact, you've been there. It's right where we found the passage to Dr. Mold's cell."

"I knew it!" Michael exclaimed. "We have to go back to that section."

We quickly followed Arthur back to where we'd found the secret passage. Flying high above the ground, this time I noticed the metal sign that hung above the shelves that read, "Hydraulics." I hadn't seen it before.

"Now do you all get it?" Michael asked expectantly.

"Um, no," Tyler said. "Stop leading us on this wild goose chase, and just tell us what you know already!"

"If Dr. Mold designed the fountains in the baron's garden, that means that medicine wasn't his only interest," Michael explained. "He must have been interested in hydraulics, too. That's the study of water forces. He would have spent time in this section of the library when he was doing his research. I think he might have hidden the formula we're looking for around here. Arthur, how many books are there in this section?"

"Around fifteen hundred," Arthur replied.

I gulped and exchanged a worried glance with Tyler. That was A LOT of books.

"All right then, what are we waiting for?" Michael said. He started pulling old books and documents off the shelf. "Let's start looking."

"Wait a minute!" Arthur interrupted. "The library will be closing in an hour, and no one, including me, will be allowed to stay after that. The director had a new infrared alarm system installed, and we start using it today!"

"Come on then," Michael insisted. "What are we waiting for? There's no time to waste!"

Are you good at math? What's 1,500 books divided by four humans and a bat, then divided by sixty minutes?

I'll tell you the answer — not enough time! When the security guard arrived to tell us the library was closing and it was time to set the alarm, no one had found the formula. In fact, we still had mountains of books to go through!

We had no choice but to leave, though. We were forced to abandon our search and follow the security guard to the main door. We had just reached the entrance hall when Arthur suddenly changed direction and slipped into a tiny utility room under the main staircase.

I looked at the security guard. He was distracted! After a moment of hesitation, Michael, Tyler, and I hid in the closet too. We were packed like sardines in a can! Dr. Black quickly ducked out of sight behind a pillar.

"We can wait in here until the security guard leaves," Arthur whispered when he saw our puzzled faces.

A few moments later, we heard the footsteps of the security guard leaving the library.

"Now what?" Tyler asked. "We still don't have a way to get back to the secret passageway. And I don't know about you guys, but I don't want to spend the night in this closet!"

"There might still be a way," Michael said. "Hey, Echo . . ."

What do you know! As usual, I was Michael's solution!

"Tyler," Michael said, "do you still have those infrared goggles in your backpack?"

"Yes," Tyler replied. "Why? What do you need them for?"

"Echo could use them to avoid the infrared sensors and keep looking for the formula," Michael explained. "I think there are only two

hundred books left to check. What do you say, Echo? Are you up for it?"

By my grandpa's sonar! How was I going to look through two hundred heavy hardcover books all by myself?

But what could I do? I was our only hope. So I put on Tyler's goggles and flew back to the section guarding the secret passageway, dodging the infrared sensors the whole time. An hour later, I sent my friends a single, short text message:

"GOT IT!"

Chapter 15

Mold-Flavored Concoctions

I quickly flew back to where my friends were waiting for me. I waved the piece of paper I'd found like a flag. After all, as my great-grandfather always used to say, "You may be small and not very tall, but your brain is as big as an oil rig!"

I handed over the formula, and Dr. Black began to read it. His face lit up with excitement. "This is it!" he exclaimed. "This is the cure!"

Suddenly, a greenish figure wearing tattered, moldy clothes appeared and jumped at him, screaming at the top of his lungs. "Rodrigooo!" the ghost yelled. "You traitor! How could you pull such an awful trick on me?"

"Calm down, Uncle Allen!" Dr. Black said. "My name is Neil Black the third, I mean . . . Allen Bick the third. I'm your great-nephew!" He tried to pull out his wallet to show his uncle some identification. "I can explain!"

But the ghost didn't listen. "And what exactly do you intend to explain?" he yelled angrily. "What a double-crossing snake you are? May your ears fall off!"

"We found your journal!" Dr. Black said quickly. "We know the truth about what really happened with Rodrigo and the baron's daughter. And we found the formula you've been looking for!" He held out the piece of paper I had just found to show his uncle.

Dr. Mold snatched the paper out of his nephew's hands and stared at it in shock. He slowly sank down on the floor, still staring intently at that worn piece of paper.

"I have been searching for this formula for more than three hundred years!" he whispered. He gazed up at us in disbelief. "Where did you find it?"

"It doesn't matter anymore," Dr. Black replied. "All that matters is that we've found it. But we need your help. You have to help us prepare this medicine. Will you?"

"Why should I?" Dr. Mold grumbled. "Greta is safe now. Rodrigo is rich and famous! What's the point now?"

"The point is my friend Becca needs your help!" I exclaimed.

Dr. Mold stared at me in shock. I don't know why you humans are always so surprised to find out I can talk!

Before Dr. Mold could respond, his nephew spoke up. "Listen to me, Uncle Allen," he said. "If you help me prepare this medicine, you'll be saving a little girl's life. And I give you my word that I'll do everything I can to let the world know what really happened to you. Everyone will know that you were the one who found the cure for blue disease, not Rodrigo."

The ghost hesitated at first, but he finally nodded. "All right," he agreed. "I'll help you. Let us go to my laboratory. All the ingredients we'll need are in there. Are you familiar with the secret passage?"

"We are, but we might have a tough time getting there," Michael said, speaking up for the first time. "The library has updated its security a bit since you lived here. They put in a new infrared security system. We can't get to the passageway without setting off the alarm."

"Don't worry," I said, pulling Tyler's infrared goggles back down over my eyes. "Leave that part to me."

"Rather clever, that flying rat of yours!" Dr. Mold said. With that he turned and started making his way down the dark hallways of the library.

Flying rat! I would have set Dr. Mold straight, but there was no time to waste. We had to get that cure to Becca.

Dr. Mold and I led the way back to the secret passageway. With the infrared goggles I could show my friends how to dodge the sensors along the way.

Once we were inside the laboratory, Dr. Bick and Dr. Mold immediately got down to business. It was like watching a scene straight out of a science-fiction movie! The old ghost helped his young nephew mix together the mysterious ingredients that had been sitting on his lab shelves for centuries.

When the medicine was finally ready, Dr. Mold turned to his great-nephew. "This should do the trick," he said. "Give the patient one teaspoon every hour for the next six hours. She should be cured by tomorrow."

Dr. Black nodded. "Thank you for your help, uncle," he said gratefully. "I couldn't have done it without you."

With the cure complete, we hurried back to Becca's room to give her the first dose. I crossed my wings that it would work!

No one got any sleep that night. Michael, Tyler, and I, along with Dr. Black, stayed up all night to make sure Becca drank every last drop of the medicine Dr. Mold had created.

It was no easy task. Becca drank the entire potion, but every time she took a sip, she exclaimed, "Yuck! It tastes like mold!"

Chapter 16

Text Messages from the Grave

The next day was Sunday. As soon as she woke up from her restless night, Becca asked Dr. Black for a mirror. Holding her breath, Becca looked at her reflection.

What a relief! Dr. Mold's potion had worked! Becca could finally see her normal face looking back at her. The nasty blue dots had completely disappeared.

You can only imagine how happy Mr. and

Mrs. Silver were to see that Becca was back to normal. They wouldn't stop kissing their daughter and thanking the doctor.

That went on until Mrs. Silver got a bit confused. She accidentally thanked Becca and kissed Dr. Black! The doctor's face immediately turned an alarming shade of red!

"We don't know how to thank you, Dr. Black," Mr. Silver said, shaking the doctor's hand. "I can't believe how quickly Becca has recovered! It's a medical miracle! However did you do it?"

"Let's just say that I had help from an old friend. I revisited a *verrrry* old remedy!" Dr. Black replied. "Sometimes those work best."

"I always say that!" Mrs. Silver agreed. "Our ancestors' remedies are still the best ones!"

Michael, Tyler, and I had to bite our tongues

to keep from laughing out loud. Mrs. Silver would be shocked if she knew just how old the ancestor and his remedy *really* were!

When everyone was finished thanking the doctor, it was time to say goodbye.

"Goodbye, Dr. Black," Michael said, shaking his hand. "Thank you again for all your help. We couldn't have done it without you. And your uncle," he added in a whisper.

"Call me Dr. Bick," the doctor replied. "I

think it's time that I start using my real name again. With my great-uncle's name cleared, I have nothing to be ashamed of."

"What are you going to do with Dr. Mold's journal?" Tyler asked.

"It's about time the world knew the truth about what Rodrigo did!" the doctor replied. "I'm going to write a book that tells the true story of what really happened. I need to redeem my great-uncle's legacy like I promised him. I just hope I can do him justice. I have to admit, I'm not a great writer."

"Echo can help you!" Tyler exclaimed. "He's an awesome writer!"

* * *

Well, what do you expect me to say? You can probably guess what happened next.

The doctor insisted that I be the one to help him write his story, and three months later, *The True Story of Dr. Mold* was published. It was an instant bestseller. Dr. Bick was thrilled. We managed to restore the old doctor's reputation once and for all.

After my friends and I returned home from our adventure, I received a very long message

from Arthur. But there was no carrier pigeon this time! This time he sent it to me using my Bat-Phone! That thing really can do everything! The message said:

Dear Echo,

Poor Gideon is just too old and tired to fly, so I finally decided it was time to buy a cell phone.

Life at Castlerock has gone back to its normal, peaceful routine since you and your friends left. Dr. Mold has stopped messing up my library, and he even returned the missing book he'd borrowed, The Science of Hydraulics.

I can't be too mad at him. He said he only borrowed it because he wanted to fix a leaky faucet in the bathrooms!

Even more exciting, the director of the library apologized for ever doubting me. My job at the library is no longer in any danger.

People here in Castlerock are still convinced that the ghost is wandering about the castle at night and wailing. But I know the truth — now that his name has been cleared, Dr. Mold has stopped searching for his missing formula. Now he prefers to stop by and have a chat with me or play cards.

We should probably keep that last part a secret, though. If word gets out that the ghost here is real, it'll be so long tourists!

By the way, Dr. Mold asked me to show him how to use a cell phone. Odd, isn't it? I wonder what he's up to.

Thank your friends for me, and please come back to visit soon!

Your old friend,

Arthur

There's nothing strange so far, right? That's what I thought at first, too. But that wasn't the last message I received on my Bat-Phone. Later that day, my phone buzzed with another message. This one read:

Hello there, my flying friend!

Based on your helpful nature at Castlerock, I had already understood what an intelligent specimen you are. But I am even more certain of it after reading the book you and my nephew wrote about me. What a wonderful read!

I cannot thank you enough for all you have

done for me. Now the whole world knows the truth about Rodrigo and what really happened.

Should you ever need the services of a good doctor (although I hope that won't be the case), please do not hesitate to summon me.

With deepest gratitude,

Allen Bick

Scaredy-bat! What would you do if you were me?

You wouldn't call him, would you?

A spooky goodbye,

Echo

ABOUT THE AUTHOR

Roberto Pavanello is an accomplished children's author and teacher. He currently teaches Italian at a local middle school and is an expert in children's theater. Pavanello has written many children's books, including *Dracula and the School of Vampires, Look I'm Calling the Shadow Man!*, and the Bat Pat series, which has been published in Spain, Belgium, Holland, Turkey, Brazil, Argentina, China, and now the United States as Echo and the Bat Pack. He is also the author of the Oscar & Co. series, as well as the Flambus Green books. Pavanello currently lives in Italy with his wife and three children.

GLOSSARY

cure (KYUR) — a drug or course of treatment that makes someone better

formula (FOR-myuh-luh) — a rule in science or math that is written with numbers and symbols

legacy (LEG-uh-see) — something handed down from one generation to another

physician (fuh-ZISH-uhn) — someone with a medical degree who has been trained and licensed to treat injured and sick people; a doctor

remedy (REM-uh-dee) — something that relieves pain, cures a disease, or corrects a disorder

technology (tek-NOL-uh-jee) — the use of science and engineering to do practical things, such as make businesses and factories more efficient

DISCUSSION QUESTIONS

1. I'm always the one risking my wings on our adventures! This time, I had to fly through a maze of infrared sensors to get back to the library. Can you think of any other ways we could have gotten there?

2. Rodrigo stole Dr. Mold's formula and took all the credit for curing Greta. Talk about why you think he would do such a thing.

3. Dr. Black was determined to clear his uncle's name. Why do you think it was so important for him to do so? Talk about it.

WRITING PROMPTS

1. I used to live in the old library at Castlerock. Write about where you grew up. What do you remember about it?

2. My old friend Arthur and I kept in touch by writing letters, at least before I got my Bat-Phone! Try writing a letter to one of your friends.

3. Imagine that Dr. Black asked you to help write *The True Story of Dr. Mold.* How would you start? Write the first chapter.

Check out more

Mysteries and Adventures with Echo and the Bat Pack

Echo and the Bat Pack
THE CHILLY MAMMOTH
Roberto Pavanello
Echo and the Bat Pack
THE DANCING VAMPIRE
Roberto Pavanello
Echo and the Bat Pack
THE PIRATE WITH THE GOLDEN TOOTH
Roberto Pavanello

THE FUN DOESN'T STOP HERE!

Discover more:

Videos & Contests

Games & Puzzles

Heroes & Villains

Authors & Illustrators

www.capstonekids.com

Find cool websites and more books like this one at www.facthound.com.

Just type in the Book ID: 9781434238344

and you're ready to go!